# The Daydreamer

David Wharry

## Series Editor: John McRae

Nelson

**Exercises and a glossary can be found at the back of the book.**

Thomas Nelson and Sons Ltd
Nelson House Mayfield Road
Walton-on-Thames Surrey
KT12 5PL UK

51 York Place
Edinburgh
EH1 3JD UK

Thomas Nelson (Hong Kong) Ltd
Toppan Building 10/F
22A Westlands Road
Quarry Bay Hong Kong

First published by Thomas Nelson and Sons Ltd 1993

ISBN 0-17-5569821
NPN 9 8 7 6 5 4 3 2 1

Illustrations by Keith Smith

Printed in Hong Kong

# Chapter 1

# Sea, Sun and Sand

*Suddenly, George hears an aeroplane. He jumps out of the jeep, runs, and throws himself flat on the sand. The aeroplane fires at the jeep. It explodes in a ball of fire.*

*The aeroplane flies round in a circle and comes back again. It comes past very low. George sees the enemy pilot look down at him and wave, smiling. He watches the aeroplane fly away into the deep blue sky.*

*A big cloud of black smoke is rising from the burning jeep. George looks around him and sees only sand, a sea of sand, everywhere as far as the eye can see. There is nothing but empty desert for hundreds of miles in every direction. He is alone. He has no water. He looks up at the burning sun. 'How many hours before I die?' ...*

Doreen Plumb, George's wife, looks up at the dark grey clouds. She turns to George, who is sitting next to her.

'George, it's going to rain.'

George doesn't hear Doreen. He is thousands of miles away, in the middle of the Sahara Desert ...

*... He can see the sea, far away, between the desert and the sky. He can see boats on the water. He laughs – he knows the sea is only a <u>mirage</u>. It is the heat that turns the sand into sea.*

*Either he stays where he is and dies of thirst, or he walks and dies of thirst. He decides to walk ...*

'George, wake up!' Doreen says loudly. 'It's going to rain!' ...

*... As he walks he talks to himself. 'There's always hope! Keep walking! If you stop you will die! Think of Doreen and the children! Think of them on the beach at Bournemouth! You will see them again! You'll swim with them in the cold grey sea! Keep walking!' ...*

Doreen gets up. She shakes George's arm. 'Don't just sit there, George!'

George looks up at Doreen. 'What did you say, dear?'

'It's beginning to rain, George!'

A drop of rain falls on George's head. He looks up and sees the dark clouds. He looks around him. People are leaving the beach in a hurry. He gets up.

'We're going to have the same weather as last year,' Doreen says as she dresses Sharon, their four-year-old daughter. 'Why do we always have to go on holiday in May?'

George sighs. 'You know why, Doreen.'

George is a house painter. He works for a big company. His boss makes him take his holidays in May instead of June, July or August. The company is always very busy during the summer months. They paint the outsides of buildings while the weather is good. Doreen is a nurse. She works in one of the hospitals in Birmingham, the city where they live.

George opens their umbrella. 'Hey, Kevin!' he shouts. Their nine-year-old son is playing with another boy. He looks round. 'Come along, son. We're going back to the hotel for lunch.'

The Plumbs walk across the beach and up the steps to the road. It is the first day of their summer holiday in Bournemouth, on the south coast of England. They have come there for a week in May for the last six years.

'The weather's better than yesterday,' George says as they shake the wet sand out of their shoes. 'It will be brighter this afternoon, you wait and see.'

'You always look on the bright side of everything, don't you, George?' Doreen says. 'You're right. The weather *is* better. Yesterday it rained *all* day.'

George is right. The rain stops as they are finishing

lunch. Far away, over the sea, blue sky appears.

'Let's go to the beach, Mum,' Kevin says, pressing his nose against the dining-room window. He breathes on the glass and draws a smiling sun with his finger.

A thin woman with a long hard face comes into the dining-room. She is Mrs Craddock, the owner of the small hotel where they stay every year.

'Hey, you!' she shouts. 'Look what you've done to my nice clean window!'

'Kevin, stop that!' George says. 'Sorry, Mrs Craddock,' he says with a friendly smile. 'Kevin is always drawing and painting. He never stops. He's top of his class in art. He won a prize ...'

Mrs Craddock sees her dog eating something under the table. 'Who dropped all these pieces of sausage? A whole sausage!' She looks at Sharon.

'I did,' Sharon replies. 'I don't like sausage and I don't like your food. It tastes horrible.'

Mrs Craddock's mouth opens wide with shock.

'And your dog eats too much,' Sharon says. 'My mother says he's too fat.'

Mrs Craddock's mouth opens even wider. Her face goes red. She looks at Doreen, turns round and walks out of the room. George and Doreen look at each other, trying hard not to laugh.

'Let's go to the beach,' George says.

Doreen looks out of the window. She is not sure

about the weather. There are still a lot of dark clouds.

'Why don't we go to the cinema?' she says. 'It will be warmer – and drier.'

'Oh no, Mum!' Kevin shouts. 'The beach!'

Doreen looks at the children, then at George, and sighs. 'The beach, the beach. That's what we always do – go to the beach, go to the beach … My husband sits and daydreams, I sit and read, and the children play.'

'The beach! Please, Mum!' says Sharon.

'We can go to the cinema tonight,' says George.

Doreen smiles. 'Three against one … as usual. Oh, all right then. Let's go.'

They go to their car, which is parked outside the hotel. They laugh about what Sharon said about Mrs Craddock's cooking as they get the things they need for the beach: chairs, a large beach umbrella for the sun, and the children's toys. They keep them in the car because Mrs Craddock says they bring too much sand into her hotel.

George lifts up the driver's seat and takes an envelope from underneath it. It is full of money. He takes out two five-pound notes.

'Why do you keep the money there, George?'

'It's safer than leaving it in the hotel.'

'Mrs Craddock may be a nasty old bag of bones,

George, but she's honest.'

George looks under the car. There is a little pool of oil on the road underneath the engine. 'The man who sold me this car wasn't honest,' he says. 'He told me it had only done 12,000 miles.'

He locks the car. 'At least he smiled when he sold it to me. Mrs Craddock never smiles, does she?'

'George?'

'What?'

'I haven't seen you smile very much lately, either. Smile!'

George smiles. Then, as he locks the car, it starts raining again. Doreen looks back at the hotel and sees Mrs Craddock cleaning the dining-room window, watching them.

'Let's wait in the car,' she says.

Everybody gets in. They wait ten, twenty minutes … until there is steam on the inside of the windows. Kevin starts drawing pictures with his finger. George watches him in the mirror. A few weeks ago, Kevin's art teacher telephoned George. He said he thought Kevin should go to art school.

Thirty minutes … Sharon falls asleep, then Kevin … Doreen reads … George watches the rain running down the windscreen …

*… The rain. It never stops. It has rained for six years without stopping. Most of the world is now under water. There is war everywhere because there is hardly any*

*space left in the world: just mountains, the tops of hills, the roofs of very high buildings. People are killing each other for dry land. New York is like Venice now – it has water instead of streets, the roofs of the big buildings have been made into vegetable farms. Meat is a problem. There are no more sheep or cows, only cats and dogs – which are made into sausages …*

It is raining harder and harder. Doreen looks up from her book. 'This isn't my idea of a holiday, George. I want to go somewhere different next year – somewhere sunny and warm.'

George does not reply. Doreen looks at him. He's staring at the windscreen …

*… George and Doreen and the children are living on top of the chimney of a factory. The factory had three chimneys, a hundred feet high, but the other two fell down – the water washed them away. Their chimney could fall down at any moment. George looks down. He was always afraid of heights, of falling … The water is only twenty feet below them, rising all the time. He is afraid of drowning now. They have no boat. A man sold him a boat with a hole in the bottom. It sank …*

'Hey, Mr Daydreamer! I'm talking to you.'

George still does not reply. Doreen switches on the windscreen wipers. George jumps and looks at Doreen.

'George, didn't you hear what I said?'

'No dear.'

'You were daydreaming.'

'Was I?'

'Yes. You were miles away. Where were you?'

George thinks for a moment. 'I can't remember.'

'I said I don't want to come to Bournemouth again next year.'

'Why not?' George says, surprised.

'Six years is enough. We need a change, George.'

'Why? What's wrong with Bournemouth? The children love the beach.'

'Bournemouth isn't the only beach in the world.'

'I didn't say it was, dear.'

Doreen closes her eyes, sighs, and shakes her head.

'You know what your problem is, don't you, George? You're happy anywhere. You're happy just sitting here daydreaming in this car, aren't you?'

'Well, I'm not *unhappy*, dear. We're on holiday.'

Doreen laughs. 'You call this a holiday!'

'A few minutes' rain isn't the end of the world, is it?'

Doreen looks at George, suddenly angry. 'It's a waste of time talking to you.' She switches off the windscreen wipers. 'Go on, go back to your daydream!'

'Hey, look!' says George. 'A rainbow. And

there's blue sky over there. It's going to stop raining. I knew it would.'

# Chapter 2

# Castles in Spain

On the way to the beach, Doreen goes into a bookshop. She buys a travel magazine. George is looking at the books in the window when she comes out.

'Buy something to read on the beach, George.'

'No thanks, dear. I'll just sit and daydream.' He looks at Doreen. 'That's all I ever do, isn't it?'

Doreen takes his arm. 'What do you mean?'

'You're right, Doreen. I never do anything. All I ever do is sit and dream about doing things.'

Doreen kisses him. 'George … you don't understand. I love you because you *are* a dreamer. There's nothing wrong with dreaming. People always dream about doing things they can't do.'

'Yes, because dreaming doesn't cost anything. You need money to do things.'

'Let's dream abut money, then.'

They stop outside a cinema and look at photographs of the film, *The Big Sleep*, with Robert Mitchum.

'It looks like a good film,' says Doreen. 'I like

14

Robert Mitchum.'

'It's a good story. I read the book,' George says.

'Tell me the story, Dad,' says Kevin.

'I can't, Kevin. It's too long. It's about a private detective in Los Angeles.'

Doreen smiles, remembering something. She takes George's arm.

'Do you remember, George?'

'Do I remember what, dear?'

'That night.'

'What night?'

'The first time we went out together.'

George smiles, remembering.

'You forgot your money,' Doreen says. 'Remember? You left it at home. We arrived at the cinema and you had no money.'

George laughs softly. 'You wanted to pay for us. But I didn't let you.'

'So we didn't see the film. You made me laugh so much.'

'Did I? Why?'

'The photographs, remember? We stood in the entrance of the cinema and looked at the photos of the film. You invented a funny story, just by looking at the photos. I stood there for an hour listening to you. It was better than seeing the film! You're such a good storyteller, George.'

'I remember something else. It was the first time

we kissed – in front of the film photographs. Remember?'

'Of course I remember! It was raining – like today!'

They kiss. The two children watch.

'I told you a lie, Doreen. I didn't forget my money.'

'I knew that, George. I didn't mind.'

They laugh. Then George is suddenly serious. He looks out at the sea, thinking about something. 'And I don't have enough money now,' he says.

'I've got enough money for the cinema,' Doreen says. She opens her bag.

'No, Doreen, I didn't mean that,' George says, shutting her bag. She looks at him.

'What do you mean, then?'

'Oh … nothing.'

'Tell me, George.'

'I'll tell you later, dear. Come on, let's go to the beach.'

Doreen watches the children playing in the sand while she reads about holidays in Spain. On the cover of the magazine there is a photograph of a beautiful woman standing next to a large silver car. There are palm trees along the road and a white castle on top of a hill.

Kevin and Sharon are making a big sandcastle.

Kevin runs to his mother and asks her to help them.

'No, I'm reading, Kevin,' Doreen says. 'Ask your father. He'll help.'

Kevin goes to his father. 'Dad, Mum says you'll help us make the castle.'

But his father does not hear him. He is thousands of miles away, in Los Angeles.

'Dad?'

George looks away from the sea to his son. 'What did you say, Kevin?'

'Will you help us with the castle, Dad?'

'Not now, son.'

'But you're not doing anything, Dad.'

'Yes I am. I'm thinking. I'll come and help you later.'

'Promise, Dad.'

'I promise, son.'

Kevin goes back to the castle. George goes back to his daydream …

*… It's hot, too hot. He gets up from his desk and goes to the window. Three o'clock in the afternoon and the street is almost empty. Everyone in Los Angeles is at the beach.*

*The phone rings. He answers it.*

*'George Plumb, private detective?' says a smooth female voice.*

'*Yes.*'

'*I will be at your office in twenty minutes, Mr Plumb.*'
The woman hangs up.

*Twenty minutes later, a very large, very expensive
silver car stops outside George's office building. A very
beautiful young woman, wearing very expensive clothes,
gets out. Standing under a palm tree, she tells the driver
to wait ...*

Doreen looks up from her magazine. A boy is
helping Kevin and Sharon build the castle. They
have almost finished. She turns to George. 'Let's go
to Spain next year, George.'

*... George hears footsteps outside his office door. The
door opens. A woman enters. George knows who she is.
She is Gloria Fanderbelt.*

*Everyone knows who Gloria Fanderbelt is. She is
often on the covers of magazines. Her father, Carter
Fanderbelt, is one of the richest men in the world ...*

'George?'

*... Gloria Fanderbelt smiles, sits down, and takes a long
cigarette from a silver case ...*

'George!' Doreen shouts. 'Listen to me!'
George jumps out of his daydream. 'Er ... What,

dear?'

'I said let's go to Spain next year. What do you think?'

George thinks. 'Where will we find the money to go to Spain, Doreen?'

'Holidays in Spain are cheaper than in England! A friend of mine, a nurse at the hospital, goes there every year. It's sad.'

'What's sad?'

'Her husband was a pilot. He died in an aeroplane crash.'

'Oh … yes, I remember you told me.' George goes back to Los Angeles again …

… *Gloria Fanderbelt smiles, sits down, and takes a long cigarette from a silver case. George lights it for her.*

*'What can I do for you, Miss Fanderbelt?'*

*Their eyes meet.*

*'Mr Plumb, I'm going to Spain this afternoon – for a short holiday. My father has a castle there.'*

*'I need a holiday too, Miss Fanderbelt. I'm tried of sitting in this chair all day long.'*

*'I want you to come to Spain with me, Mr Plumb.'*

*'Let's go,' George says, smiling.*

*Gloria Fanderbelt gives him a long cold look. 'Mr Plumb, I want you to investigate a mystery.'*

'A mystery?'

'My brother died in Spain two months ago. My father gave him an aeroplane for his birthday. The first time he flew the aeroplane, he crashed into my father's castle.'

'Dad! Dad, look!'

'What's so mysterious about that, Miss Fanderbelt?'

'Dad! Dad!' Kevin runs up to George.

'Mr Plumb, I don't believe my brother is dead.'
'Why?'
'The aeroplane was empty when it crashed.'

'Dad! My friend's aeroplane crashed into our castle! It's ruined! Help us build it again, Dad. Please!'

Doreen looks at George. He is looking at the ruined sandcastle, with the toy aeroplane lying beside it. 'Leave your father alone, Kevin. He's tired.'

... Yes, he is tired. He needs a holiday. So he goes to Spain with Gloria. He likes Spain – it is not as hot as Los Angeles. And Gloria is right – her brother is not dead.

George searches for him in every city in Europe. One day, in Vienna, he meets the mysterious Mr Arcady. He knows where Gloria's brother is.

'*He is working on a sheep farm in Australia, Mr Plumb.*'

*The next day, George leaves Amsterdam on a boat for Australia. Every day, in the ship's dining-room, he sees a beautiful woman. He cannot stop looking at her.*

*One day, as the ship is passing Sicily, he sits next to her at lunch. They talk. Her name is Doreen. She is going to live in Australia.*

'*I've always wanted to go and live in Australia, too,*' *George says.* '*I'm going to stay there after I have found Gloria's brother.*'

'*Who is Gloria?*' *Doreen says suddenly.*

'*Oh … just someone I know.*'

*As they are going through the Suez Canal, George tells Doreen he loves her. One starry night, in the middle of the Indian Ocean, Doreen tells George she loves him. The ship stops in Singapore. There, in a taxi, George asks Doreen to marry him. She says yes.*

*East of Java, near the island of Krakatoa, there is a big storm. The ship hits rocks and sinks.*

*But George and Doreen do not sink with it. For a day and a night they float in the ocean, holding on to one of the ship's chairs.*

*The next morning they see land.*

'*It's Australia!*' *Doreen says. But the chair is getting heavier and heavier. They are slowly sinking …*

23

It is late in the afternoon. The beach is nearly empty. The <u>tide</u> has come up. The water has destroyed the <u>sandcastle</u>.

When George opens his eyes he sees nothing but sea. His feet are cold. He looks down at them. They are in the water. His chair is in the water. He hears Doreen and the children laughing behind him.

Doreen takes a photograph of George sitting in the sea.

# Chapter 3

# The Man with his Head in the Clouds

Later, after supper, George watches the news on television. Kevin sits with his mother. Sharon is already in bed, asleep.

Kevin watches Doreen writing crosses next to the names of football teams.

'What are you doing, Mum?'

'I'm doing the football pools, dear.'

'What's the football pools?'

'It's a game. Every week, you have the list of next week's football games. You put a cross next to a team if you think it will win.'

'How do you know which team will win, Mum?'

'I don't know, dear. I don't know anything about football. I put crosses anywhere. I don't even look at the names of the teams. But you can win a lot of money if you guess correctly.'

'Dad knows a lot about football. Why doesn't he do the football pools for you?'

'He says it's a waste of time. Here, you try it.' She hands Kevin the sheet of paper. Kevin does not take it. He is watching the television news.

An elephant is with its baby, by a river. The mother is blowing water over the little one. There is the sound of gunshot. The mother elephant falls down dead. Men walk up to her dead body. They push the baby elephant away and start to cut off the mother's tusks.

Doreen looks round at Kevin and sees tears in his eyes.

The news ends with the weather forecast. 'Look, Doreen,' George says. 'It's going to be a nice day tomorrow. They say it will be good weather all week.'

'I'll believe it when I see it,' Doreen replies.


Next morning, when Doreen opens her eyes, she sees bright yellow squares on the curtains. She gets out of bed and pulls the curtains back. Sunlight pours into the room. She opens the window and breathes the fresh morning air. There isn't a cloud in the sky; the sea is shining like silver.

'George, I can't believe it!'

George wakes up with a jump. 'What, dear?' he says, half asleep.

'Look! It's a fine day.'

They get dressed, have breakfast and go straight to the beach. When they arrive it is already crowded.

Doreen lies on the airbed and sunbathes, George sits in his chair and daydreams, and the children play in the sand.

Doreen opens one eye and looks at George. 'A penny for your thoughts, dear.'

'I'm thinking about the clouds.'

Doreen looks up at the sky, suddenly worried.

'There aren't any clouds, George.'

'I mean the clouds I painted on the wall, dear.'

'Oh ... yes,' Doreen replies.

Before they went on holiday, George did a special job. He painted a blue sky and clouds on the wall of a factory near Birmingham.

It was a very big wall. The job took three weeks to finish. Before George started, an artist came to draw the lines around the clouds. He and George had lunch together.

During the three weeks, the artist often came back to see the work. He and George talked a lot. A reporter came and photographed George painting the clouds. The photograph was in a newspaper, with the words: 'George Plumb, the man with his head in the clouds'.

'It was hard work, but I enjoyed it,' George says. 'It was the first time I've ever done anything artistic. I had a lot of time to think, alone up there, painting those clouds.'

Doreen is watching Sharon playing. She is on her

own, playing with her dolls in the sand, talking to them.

'Sharon is just like you, George,' Doreen says. 'Look at her with her dolls. She sits there for hours in another world, a dream world of her own.'

George smiles. 'It's a real world for her.'

An aeroplane flies past over the sea, pulling a long flag behind it. On the flag is written: 'Visit Bournemouth Zoo'.

'I wish that stupid aeroplane would stop flying up and down the beach,' George says.

'It only goes past once a day,' says Doreen. 'Look! The pilot's waving again. He waved yesterday too.'

George looks to his left and sees a group of people waving. 'Maybe that's his family over there.'

'Let's go to the zoo this afternoon, George. The kids love it.'

'We went last year, Doreen, and the year before.'

'What's wrong with you, George? You never want to do anything any more.'

George does not reply.

'Say something, George.'

'What do you want me to say?'

'I don't know! You never say anything, George. You never do anything. You just sit there like a piece of stone. What's wrong with you?'

29

'I've got a lot of things to think about, Doreen.'

'What things?'

'I'll tell you later.'

'Are you thinking about Australia again?'

'No, I'm not.'

George and Doreen have always wanted to go and live in Australia.

'Australia is just a dream, Doreen. All I do is talk about it – it's just hot air.'

'Dreams can come true, George – if you want them to. You have to make them come true.'

George gets up suddenly. 'I'm going for a swim.'

Doreen looks at him, very surprised. 'I must be dreaming! You haven't been for a swim for years, George!'

'Well I'm going for one now. Give me the airbed, will you?'

George's idea of a swim is to float on the airbed. He lies on his back, looking up at the sky. There are one or two clouds now. He is floating like a cloud …

… *Floating over Africa in a hot-air balloon. He looks down and sees wild animals: zebras, giraffes, lions, crocodiles, elephants. He sees a dead elephant. Men are cutting off its tusks. Ivory hunters …*

The aeroplane flies past again, above George. 'Visit

Bournemouth Zoo'.

*… George looks down from his aeroplane and waves at Doreen and the children. They are standing outside their house in Australia. Australia is very big. You have to go everywhere in an aeroplane instead of a car.*

*He flies over the Australian Desert. It is such a long way to go to work every day. He sees a large cloud of black smoke below. He flies lower. A jeep is burning. He flies even lower. A man is standing beside the jeep … It's him! George Plumb! Himself!*

*Standing in the middle of the desert, George waves at himself flying past in the aeroplane above. He can't believe his eyes. How can he be in two places at the same time? How can he be two people? He knows why. He always wanted to be a pilot, up there in the clouds … The pilot is the other George Plumb, the George Plumb he will never be …*

*He wakes up. Was he daydreaming? No, he was asleep. How long was he asleep? He rubs his eyes and gets up.*

*'You slept for four years, thirty-two days and fourteen hours, sir,' says Spaceman Digby, standing next to him. 'It will be another three years before we reach Space Station Fourteen. Would you like a cup of tea?'*

*He looks out of the window, at the millions of stars. They are three million light years away from Earth …*

'George. Here's your cup of tea.'

George wakes up. He looks around him. He is sitting in an armchair in the living-room of the hotel. It is raining outside. What happened? How did he get here?

He remembers. After lunch they went to the zoo. It started to rain so they came back to the hotel.

Doreen hands him his cup of tea.

# Chapter 4

# Blue

The next morning, Doreen wakes up first again. She gets out of bed and pulls the curtain back – grey sky, grey sea. She looks down at the street below and breathes in suddenly. Her eyes open wide, her mouth opens.

'George!'

*… George and Doreen are living in Australia. They are very happy. George is rich. He owns a business. His company paints clouds on the walls of factories.*

*George has a new aeroplane. They fly out of the city in it, along the coast. George's aeroplane is pulling a long flag behind it. On the flag is written: 'George Plumb, the Man with his Head in the Clouds.'*

*'Where are we going, George?' Doreen asks.*

*'It's a surprise,' George replies.*

*An hour later, George lands beside a beautiful sandy beach. His car is waiting. They drive away. A few minutes later, George turns off the road. He drives through a tall gate into a large green garden, past a swimming pool, a tennis court. They stop in front of a*

*big white house.*

'Who lives here, dear?' Doreen asks.

'We do. I bought it for us yesterday.'

*They go inside and look around the empty rooms. There are beautiful views from every window. The children run out and play in the garden. George and Doreen go upstairs. They walk through the bedrooms.*

'*I can't believe it, George,*' *Doreen says.* '*This is a dream come true.*' *She goes into the next room.* '*This will be our bedroom.*' *She goes to the window and looks out.*

'George, look!' *she says …*

George wakes up suddenly. He sees Doreen standing by the window.

'George! Look!'

'What, dear?'

'The car!'

'The car? What's happened to it?'

'It's not there any more! It's gone!'

George runs downstairs and out into the street. He looks at the empty space where the car was. He looks in either direction. Did he move it yesterday? No. It was stolen during the night.

'The money!'

Doreen comes outside. 'Now what are we going to do?'

'I don't know. Go to the police station, I suppose.'

Two hours later, on his way back from the police station, George sits down on a bench. He holds his head in his hands and thinks.

'I've lost everything – the car, all our money. I have nothing in the bank – just a few pounds.' He laughs to himself. 'Perhaps it will be easier to start again. It will be easier to start a new life with nothing. I'll have nothing to lose ...'

'Come on, let's go and pack our suitcases,' George says when he arrives back at the hotel.

'Why?' Doreen says. 'We can stay until the end of the week, can't we? You paid Mrs Craddock when we arrived.'

'She said I could pay her at the end of the week ...'

Doreen closes her eyes. She doesn't say anything.

'Yes,' George says. 'All our money was in the car. The only thing to do is go back to Birmingham.'

Doreen opens her eyes and thinks. 'I'm sure Mrs Craddock will let us stay. I'll phone my father. He'll send us some money.'

'No, Doreen. We're going back to Birmingham. I've got things to do there.'

'What things? We're on holiday.'

'Dad?' Kevin says. 'Will the police find the car?'

'I hope so, son. I'm going to sell it if they do.'

'Sell it?' says Doreen. 'Why? We only bought it two weeks ago.'

'I'll tell you later. Come on, let's go and pack.'

They promise to pay Mrs Craddock at the end of the month. She lends them money to take a train. Mr Craddock takes them to the station in his car.

Just before Birmingham, the train passes a very large factory. Clouds of white smoke are coming out of the three tall chimneys. The long blue wall has clouds painted on it.

'It's your wall, Dad!' Kevin shouts.

'It's beautiful, George,' Doreen says.

'Is that where they make the clouds, Dad?' Sharon says. George and Doreen laugh.

'Yes, my little one,' George says. 'And every cloud has a silver lining.'

Looking at George's wall, Kevin says, 'Dad, when you were a boy, what did you want to be when you grew up?'

'I wanted to be a pilot. I wanted to fly, up there in the clouds. I wanted to see the world.'

'I want to be an artist when I grow up. I want to paint pictures, big pictures that everybody will see.'

'You can paint pictures for us, son.'

'Yes. I'll paint lots of pictures for you and Mum.'

'I didn't mean for me and Mum, Kevin.'

'What do you mean, George,' Doreen says.

'Doreen, when I painted that wall, the artist and I became friends. We decided to start a business together. We'll paint pictures – they're called murals – on the outsides of buildings.'

'You need money to start a business, George. We haven't got a penny.'

'I'll find the money, Doreen. I've decided to make *this* dream come true.'

They arrive at New Street Station in Birmingham. They don't have enough money for a taxi so they take a bus. It is a long walk from the bus stop to their home and the children help to carry the suitcases.

When Doreen opens the front door of their flat, there are several letters on the floor inside. She picks them up without looking at them – she can see most of them are bills. She puts them on the kitchen table.

What are they going to eat? There is some food in tins. She sends Kevin to buy some bread.

After supper, George sits silently in front of the television, deep in thought:

'Where can I find the money to start a business? I can't sell the car – it was stolen. We'll need a van to

carry our tools. Perhaps I can borrow money from the bank. I'll go tomorrow and ask.'

There is a programme about ancient Egypt on TV. A man is standing in front of a pyramid, talking about the Pharoahs. The Pharoahs were the kings of ancient Egypt. They built the pyramids as tombs. They were buried in them with all their treasure … All the Pharoahs' tombs were robbed except one: the tomb of Tutankhamen …

*… It is three thousand years ago, in ancient Egypt. The Pharoah is building a pyramid. It is nearly finished. When it is finished it will be painted white. The Pharoah asks George to paint it.*

*'White will be too bright in the sun, Pharoah. I think blue will be better. I can paint it exactly the same colour as the sky.'*

*'Then nobody will see my pyramid!'*

*'Exactly, Pharoah. Nobody will know where your tomb is. Nobody will rob it. Your treasure will be safe for ever.'*

*'A very good idea, George …'*

*'I can paint clouds on the blue if you want.'*

*'There are never any clouds in the desert.'*

*'Of course … I forgot.'*

*'Blue. A good idea. You have the job, George. You must use the best paint money can buy. I want my*

pyramid to look beautiful for thousands of years after I die. The paint factory is a long way away, in Cairo. You can bring the paint to the pyramid by boat, on the river Nile.'

'It will be quicker by road, Pharoah. But my car was stolen. I need to buy a van.'

'Car? Van? What are these foreign words?'

'I'm going to the bank tomorrow to borrow money.'

'Bank? What is a bank?'

'You're rich, Pharoah. Perhaps you can lend me the money?'

'This man is mad. Guards take him away! Throw him to the lions!' ...

'XHM 66RT. George, look!' Doreen says. 'It's our car!'

George wakes up. The news is on television. There was a bank robbery in Bournemouth. The police chased the robbers. The robbers' car crashed into a tree. It was a stolen car – George's car.

41

# Chapter 5

# Time to Wake up

George lies awake all night, thinking about the future. Next morning, he gets up early, before everybody else.

He makes a cup of tea and sits down at the kitchen table. 'I have a week before I go back to work,' he thinks. 'I must use that time to find out how to start a business.

'I need to know the price of a van. We'll need somewhere to keep our tools and the paint – there will be so many different colours. We'll have to buy so many things ... I need to know how much everything costs. I'll make a list.'

He takes an envelope from the pile of letters on the table. He opens it – the electricity bill. 'Forty three pounds for three months,' he says. 'Is that how much we pay?'

The next envelope is the telephone bill. He pushes the pile away. 'Doreen always pays the bills. She's careful with money. Perhaps she can help me with our business ...'

He starts to write a list on the back of the

electricity bill. The first thing he writes is 'bank'. He remembers the last time he went to see the bank manager. He went to borrow money to buy the car …

He thinks about his crashed car. 'They didn't have to rob a bank. There was enough money in the car! How much money have I got in the bank now? Forty, fifty pounds? Enough to pay the telephone bill …'

He remembers what his father said once: 'If you don't know how much money you have in the bank, then you're a rich man.'

He has a thought. 'How will we find work? We can't just go to every factory and ask if they want their walls painted …'

He has an idea. 'We'll advertise – like Bournemouth Zoo …'

… *We'll buy an aeroplane. I'll fly it up and down England pulling a flag. What will we write on the flag?* …

'There you go! Daydreaming again! No more daydreams, George! You must wake up if you want to start a business.'

Kevin comes into the kitchen and sees his father talking to himself. George hears him and looks round.

'Oh … you're up early, Kevin.'

'Yes, Dad. I couldn't sleep.'

'Nor could I, son.' He pours Kevin a cup of tea, and puts his hand on his son's head. 'Kevin?'

'Yes, Dad?'

'Can I take some of your drawings to show to someone?'

'Yes, Dad.'

'Thanks.'

George puts on a tie and his best jacket.

'How do I look?'

'Smart.'

'Good. Tell Mum I'm going to the bank. I'll see you later. Bye.'

'Dad?'

'What, son?'

'Good luck.'

'Thanks, Kevin, but I need more than luck.'

It is a beautiful sunny morning. George decides to walk through the park. He stops to watch the ducks on the lake.

He looks at his watch – eight-thirty. The bank opens at nine. He has time to sit down and think about what he will say to the bank manager.

A man stops to feed the ducks. It is Mr Tooth, the bank manager. 'He looks different when he's not behind his desk,' George thinks. 'He doesn't look so hard and cold.'

ials 999, the number for

ager is a smart young man with
like cold steel.

et a lot of people like you. You
rt a business, don't you?'

't think it will be easy,' George

an walk into this bank, ask for
give it to you.'

that at all. I – '

s that, Mr Plumb. First, you have
ore we will lend you any. You
have you?'

e to know how much money you
don't know, do you?'

actly, but ...'

ouse you can sell?'

ks at George's bank record. 'I
. You can sell that.'

t ... it was used for a bank

r gives George a long cold look.
s. He answers it, listens, and
oking at George very strangely.

Mr Tooth sees George and recognises him.

'Hello, Mr Plumb! How are you?'

'He remembers my name!' George thinks. 'Fine,
thanks, Mr Tooth,' he says. 'How are you?'

'Very well, thank you.' He sits down.

'He's sitting down next to me!' George thinks.
'This *is* a piece of luck!'

'How is the new car?' Mr Tooth asks.

'Er ... fine, thank you. I'm going to the bank in a
few minutes – to ask for more money!'

Mr Tooth laughs. 'Are you?'

George smiles at the surprisingly friendly bank
manager. 'Yes. I'm going to start a business.'

He tells Mr Tooth about his plans. He shows him
Kevin's drawings.

'I think it's a very good idea. I'm sure the
business will be a success. It's a pity that I don't
work at the bank any more.'

'You don't?' George says, looking very
disappointed.

'No. I retired last week. I was sixty-five on
Thursday.'

'Happy birthday,' George says.

'Don't worry, Mr Plumb,' Mr Tooth says. 'I'm
sure the new manager will agree to lend you the
money.'

Doreen clears the kitchen table as Kevin is finishing

his breakfast.

'Kevin, why don't you go out and play football this morning? It's a beautiful day.'

'No, Mum. I want to do some drawings for Dad. He can paint them on buildings.'

'That's a good idea.'

Kevin goes into the living-room and Doreen sits down to pay the bills. She looks at the electricity bill and sees that George has written the word 'bank' on the back. She opens the telephone bill, the rent bill ...

She gets up to make some more tea, opening the next envelope – it looks like a letter from the bank.

In the next room, Kevin is drawing a huge eye, with a small window in the centre. 'It will look good on the wall of a factory,' he thinks.

He hears his mother cry out. He looks into the kitchen and sees her fall to the floor. As she falls she hits her head on the corner of the table.

Kevin runs into the kitchen. There is blood on the floor beside his mother's head. She is not moving. Is she dead? He kneels down beside her. She is alive, breathing very softly.

Kevin is very afraid. He doesn't know what to do. His father said he was going to the bank. He will run to the bank. No, he must stay with his mother. She may die! He must do something!

Kevin runs into the living-room. He picks up the

He puts down the telephone.

'Have you ever been in prison, Mr Plumb?'

'No,' George replies, surprised. 'Why do you ask that?' He hears the door open behind him, looks round and sees two policemen.

'Mr Plumb,' one of them says. 'We'd like to speak to you. Will you come outside?'

'Er, yes … Is anything wrong?'

A nurse shows George into Doreen's room. Doreen is lying on the bed with her eyes closed. She looks very beautiful, very peaceful.

She has not woken up since the accident. George talked to the doctors. They are very worried about her. Machines are monitoring her heart and her breathing.

George kisses her and sits down beside her. He holds her hand. He listens to the machine monitoring her heart: *tick … tick … tick …*

An hour later, Doreen opens her eyes. Slowly, she looks round and sees George.

'George, where was I?'

'You were a long long way away, dear. I'm glad you came back.'

'I was in Australia.'

George smiles.

'We're going to go and live in Australia, George. We're rich.'

George smiles again. He takes her hand, kisses her cheek. 'Doreen, it was only a dream.'

'No it wasn't,' Doreen replies softly. Then, suddenly, she looks very worried. 'The letter, George. Where is it?'

'What letter, dear?'

'The letter from the football pools. We won the football pools, George. We won – how much? I can't remember ... Oh, my head hurts.'

'Don't worry about it, dear. You must rest.'

'I think it was £764,000.'

George laughs. 'You're worse than me! I'm the daydreamer in this family, not you!'

# Exercises and Activities

*Chapter 1*

1   What does George do? What does Doreen do? Where are the
    Plumb family? Where exactly are they when the story begins?
    Why do they return to their hotel?
    What exact words does Doreen say to George before 'a drop of
    rain falls on George's head'? Why does George not hear her?
    Where is George, in his imagination? Where is he actually? Can
    you see any connection between the two places?
    Write a letter from Doreen to a friend describing the first day of
    the holiday.

2   Use the information in chapter one to complete the following
    sentences:

    *Example:*
    *I don't like your food because it tastes horrible.*
    *Your dog eats too much, so he's too fat.*

    *a*  It starts to rain, so .....
    *b*  Mrs Craddock walks out of the room because .....
    *c*  George keeps his money in the car because .....
    *d*  Kevin should go to art school because .....
    *e*  George is afraid of drowning because .....
    *f*  Doreen wants to go somewhere different next year
         because .....
    *g*  Look! There's a rainbow and blue sky, so .....

3   When and where did the Plumb family go for their holiday last
    year? What was the weather like?
    How often do you take a holiday: every year/more
    frequently/less frequently? Do you always go to the same place
    or to different places?
    Would you prefer the opposite?

*Chapter 2*

1   Why do you think Doreen buys a travel magazine? Where do the family go? What happens to Kevin's sandcastle? Why does Doreen want to go to Spain? Why doesn't George help Kevin build his sandcastle? Do you think the Plumbs are a happy family? Why/Why not? Describe the scene at the end of the chapter in your own words.

2   Find at least four things which George is asked or told to do. Say what George actually does and why he does it:

*Examples:*
*Doreen says, 'Buy something to read'.*
*George says no, because he wants to sit and daydream.*

3   Add another sentence beginning with 'Neither' or 'So' to the following sentences. You will find the correct names in chapters one and two.

*Examples:*
*Mrs Craddock's hotel is not very nice. Neither is she.*
*Kevin wants to go to the beach. So does Sharon.*

   *a*  Mrs Craddock doesn't smile much.
   *b*  George and Doreen are living on top of a chimney.
   *c*  Doreen doesn't help build the sandcastle.
   *d*  Gloria goes to Spain.
   *e*  Kevin is playing in the sand.
   *f*  George doesn't sink with the ship.

3   George has a long daydream in this chapter. What is his job in this daydream? Describe Gloria Fanderbelt. Why does Gloria come to see George? Why does George go to Australia? Who does he meet on the boat? What happens?
    George is a daydreamer. Why do you think he daydreams? All George's daydreams are connected to what is happening in his life. What connections are there in the Gloria Fanderbelt daydream to George's life? Why do you think people daydream? What are the good things about daydreaming? What are the bad

things? Do you daydream? Be honest! Invent a daydream with another student. Then write a paragraph describing your daydream.

*Chapter 3*

1   What are the football pools? Why is Doreen doing the football pools?
    What was the special job George did in a factory in Birmingham? Why did Doreen get angry with George? Act out the scene between Doreen and George.

2   Find the following idioms and phrases. Explain them in your own words:

    – a penny for your thoughts
    – to have your head in the clouds
    – you're like a piece of stone
    – it's just hot air
    – he can't believe his eyes

    What is an idiom? Do you know any other idioms in English?

3   In chapter 3 the weather gets better. Find the phrases that tell you this.
    Put into order the following words describing the weather. Start with the best and finish with the worst:

    horrible; fair; nice; dull; wonderful; nasty.

*Chapter 4*

1   Why do the Plumb family have to return to Birmingham? What is George's reaction to this? Do you think he is still being a daydreamer?
    Why/Why not?
    What do the family hear on the news? What do you think they say to each other as they watch? Act out the scene, then write the dialogue.

2   We use the Future Simple tense when we have just decided to do

something. For example, Doreen says: 'I'll phone my father'.
She has only just decided to phone her father. Find four more
examples of this use of the Future Simple tense in this chapter.
We also use the Future Simple to predict. For example, Doreen
says: 'I'll phone my father'. Predict what you think will happen
to the Plumb family:

*Example:*
*I think they'll get back their money from the car.*

3   Find the following words and phrases and explain their meaning:

breathes in; pack; lends; pilot; murals; bills; tombs; borrow.

## Chapter 5

1   George wants to start a business. Look at the beginning of this
chapter.
What ideas does he have? How can Kevin help him? Do you
think George's plans for a business will be successful? What is
the difference between George as he is now and George as he
was? Do you like him more now? Why/Why not?

2   How many of the following characters do you remember? First
match the names with their professions:

| | |
|---|---|
| Mr Tooth | magazine model |
| Pharoah | hotel owner |
| Gloria Fanderbelt | film actor |
| Robert Mitchum | king |
| Mrs Craddock | retired bank manager |

Now say where George met these people and whether he met
them in real life or just in his daydreams.

3   Do you believe Doreen when she says they have won the football
pools?
Do you think George believes her? How do you feel now about
George?
Would you like him in your family?

# Glossary

**bag of bones**   a very thin person
**breathe(s)**   to take air into and out of the body
**chimney**   part of the roof that lets smoke out
**coast**   the land beside the sea
**daydream(s)**   to imagine pleasant stories, often about yourself
**desert**   a large sandy piece of land with very little rain
**drown(ing)**   to die by being under water for a long time
**explode(s)**   suddenly to go to pieces with a very loud noise
**factory**   building where objects are made by machines
**jeep**   a type of car that can be used off the road
**mirage**   something you see in the desert that is not actually there
**prize**   a gift for doing something well
**rainbow**   an arch of seven different colours in the sky
**space**   an area that is not used or filled
**steam**   the gas produced by boiling water
**waste of time**   it is no use; it does not help
**windscreen**   the front window of a car
**windscreen wipers**   rubber blades that remove rain from car
windows

**castle**   a large building built hundreds of years ago; used for
protection against enemies
**detective**   someone whose job is to investigate crimes
**float**   to stay on top of the water, without sinking
**investigate**   to examine something in order to discover the truth
**mystery**   something which people cannot explain or understand
**rock**   a large separate piece of stone
**ruined**   destroyed
**sink(s)**   to go under water
**tide**   the regular rise and fall of the sea, pulled by the moon

*Chapter 3*

**a penny for your thoughts**   tell me what you are thinking
**have your head in the clouds**   to be a dreamer, not a practical
person
**it's just hot air**   it's talk, not action
**ivory**   elephant tusks are made of ivory
**reporter**   someone whose job is to write about the news for a
newspaper
**space(man)**   the region beyond the earth; someone who travels in
space
**sunbathe(s)**   to stay in the sun in order to get brown
**tusk(s)**   the long white tooth that comes out of an elephant's mouth

*Chapter 4*

**accident**   when someone gets hurt, or something is broken, by
chance
**ancient**   very old
**bill**   a paper saying how much you must pay for something
**bury(ied)**   to put a dead body under the ground or in a tomb
**crash(ed)**   to go into violently
**emergency**   something bad that suddenly happens; you must deal
with it immediately
**every cloud has a silver lining**   every bad thing has something
good about it
**luck**   things that happen by chance
**monitor(ing)**   to check continuously
**mural**   a painting which is painted on a wall
**retire(d)**   to stop work because of age
**rob(bed)**   to steal something from a place or person
**steel**   a type of very hard metal
**tomb**   a stone box for a dead person
**treasure**   riches: money, gold, silver, jewellery
**van**   a vehicle used to carry things